MW00736637

PUFFIN BOOKS
THE HIDDEN POOL

For over forty-five years, Ruskin Bond has been writing stories, novellas, essays, poems and children's books. He has written over 500 short stories and articles, many of which have been published by Penguin India.

Ruskin Bond grew up in Jamnagar, Dehradun, New Delhi and Simla. As a young man, he spent four years in the Channel Islands and London. He returned to India in 1955 and has never left the country since. His first novel *The Room on the Roof* received the John Llewellyn Rhys Prize, awarded to a Commonwealth writer under thirty, for 'a work of outstanding literary merit'. He received a Sahitya Akademi Award in 1993 and the Padma Shri in 1999.

He lives in Landour, Mussoorie, with his extended family.

By the same author in Puffin

Rusty, the Boy from the Hills
Rusty Runs Away
Rusty and the Leopard
Rusty Goes to London
Rusty Comes Home
The Room on the Roof
Panther's Moon and Other Stories
Treasury of Stories for Children

The Hidden Pool

Ruskin Bond

Illustrations by
Ranjit Balmuchu

PUFFIN BOOKS

PUFFIN BOOKS
Published by the Penguin Group
Penguin Books India Pvt. Ltd, 7th Floor, Infinity Tower C, DLF Cyber City,
Gurgaon - 122 002, Haryana, India
Penguin Group (USA) Inc., 375 Hudson Street, New York, New York 10014, USA
Penguin Group (Canada), 90 Eglinton Avenue East, Suite 700, Toronto, Ontario,
M4P 2Y3, Canada
Penguin Books Ltd, 80 Strand, London WC2R 0RL, England
Penguin Ireland, 25 St Stephen's Green, Dublin 2, Ireland (a division of Penguin
Books Ltd)
Penguin Group (Australia), 707 Collins Street, Melbourne, Victoria 3008, Australia
Penguin Group (NZ), 67 Apollo Drive, Rosedale, Auckland 0632, New Zealand
Penguin Books (South Africa) (Pty) Ltd, Block D, Rosebank Office Park, 181 Jan
Smuts Avenue, Parktown North, Johannesburg 2193, South Africa

Penguin Books Ltd, Registered Offices: 80 Strand, London WC2R 0RL, England

Originally published by Children's Book Trust 1966
This edition first published in Puffin by Penguin Books India 2005

ISBN 9780143334873
Reprinted in 2014

Typeset in Sabon by Mantra Virtual Services, New Delhi
Printed at Repro India Ltd, Navi Mumbai

A PENGUIN RANDOM HOUSE COMPANY

*Dedicated to Argha Mukherjee
who has collected all my stories,
even some that I can't find!*

Contents

Contents

Preface

The Hidden Pool was my first book for children. Ten years earlier, in 1956, my first novel, *The Room on the Roof,* had been published in England; but that work, written by an adolescent, was not intended for children. Its earnest young author took himself and his subject very seriously.

In the 1950s and early '60s, children's literature in India hardly existed. There were imported books, and some writings in the regional languages, but our mainstream publishers would not take on children's books until Shankar and the Children's Book Trust came on the scene and created a 'first' in publishing for children.

The Hidden Pool was one of the first titles published by the Children's Book Trust. It appeared in 1966 in English, and in Hindi and Bengali translations. Ten years later, it was out of print except for an edition for schools.

It doesn't have much of a plot. It is simply the story of three boys who meet regularly at a secret pool outside their small town, decide on having an adventure, and set out to reach a famous glacier in Kumaon. It was based on my own trek to the Pindari Glacier when I was a boy. In those days, it was unusual for youngsters to go on long hikes or treks into the mountains, and I am glad to say that it did motivate a number of boys and girls into doing just that.

Nowadays, I find groups of school children from all over the country coming to the hills of Uttaranchal and Himachal and undertaking ambitious hikes and expeditions into the mountains. Getting away from their cities, and exploring and discovering all that the Himalayas have to offer, is a healthy and encouraging trend. Rivers and forests, remote villages, ancient temples, exotic birds, animals and flowers are still there, waiting to be discovered by my young readers in the same way that they brought pleasure and excitement to Laurie and his friends.

After *The Hidden Pool*, I was to write many books and stories for my younger readers. But this is the one that started me off.

Landour, Mussoorie   Ruskin Bond
July 2004

Spring Festival

Anil said, 'You are a snob, mister.'

'Why?' I asked.

'Because you won't play Holi. You want to shut yourself up in your house when everyone else is celebrating the coming of spring. I know, you are afraid to spoil your clothes.'

I shrugged my shoulders to let him know that he could think what he liked.

'You're afraid of your parents, that's why it is,' continued Anil. 'You are afraid of being punished for running around with bazaar people!'

'You are welcome to think so,' I said coldly.

Anil had often told me about Holi. It was not merely a Hindu festival of playing with colours, when men and women and children threw coloured dust and water on each other, when there were singing and shouting and the beating of drums; it also heralded the Hindu New Year, when Nature is born again, blossoming out in colour and music.

New colour, new music, new life. Seasons die, and seasons are born again. The colours that are thrown are an expression of joy in the new springtime of life and young love.

The Holi festival held a fascination for me. But until I was fifteen, my parents, who had brought me to India two years earlier (when my father had taken a job with a new hydroelectric project), had not allowed me to take part in the celebration. They were afraid I might get hurt in the rough play, or be lost in the bazaars. I had stayed at home, listening to the drums, the songs, and the inviting shouts of some of my school friends.

Anil's father kept a cloth shop in the bazaar, and it was in the bazaar that I had met Anil, for he went to a different school. I was walking home from the post office and did not pay much attention to the large cow that was moving leisurely through the crowd, nosing around the vegetable stalls.

A cyclist came down the road, pedalling furiously. Pedestrians scattered. I found myself beside the cow, in the middle of the road. The cyclist was faced with the choice of colliding either with me or with the cow. He chose me.

'You clumsy fellow!' I cried, picking myself up from the ground, while the cow stared sorrowfully at me.

'I'm sorry,' said the cyclist, a boy of about my age. 'I couldn't help it.'

'Why not?'

'Why not? Because if I had not bumped into you, I would have bumped into the cow!' Then, as he saw me growing indignant, he hurried on. 'Please don't misunderstand. It is not that I prefer the cow to you, but I might have broken my head if I had banged into her! She is an immovable object, and you are not!'

I could think of no retort.

A few weeks later I saw the boy again, but we were on a lonely road this time, with plenty of space in which to avoid bumping into each other; but, seeing a familiar face, the boy swerved his bicycle dangerously to the edge of the road and almost swept me off my feet.

'Oh, hello there!' he said, making sure his cycle had not been damaged. 'And how are you?'

'I'm fine,' I said, preparing to continue my walk.

The boy got into step with me and pursued the topic of my well-being. 'I hope I did not hurt you that day in the bazaar.'

'You were going the other way just now, weren't you?' I said, very rudely.

He looked disappointed but then he smiled, and there was something about his smile that made me smile too. And he said, 'Don't be so angry . . .'

'I'm not angry,' I said.

'Please don't be hurt.'

'I'm not hurt.'

'Please don't be a snob!'

This had more effect. The boy watched me with astonishment as my cheeks grew red.

'I'm not a snob! I said.

The boy grinned at me. 'Now you are angry *and* hurt! So you are not a snob . . . Good! . . . Come and have some chaat with me.'

Standing off the road was a small wooden shop, draped with sacking. I hesitated in the entrance, suspicious of the wild sweet smells, of the murmur of unfamiliar voices, of the fact that I knew nothing about the stranger who had invited me in. But to have refused would have been to invite further derision. I followed the boy into the shop.

I discovered that chaat was a spiced and sweetened mixture of different fruits and vegetables—potatoes, guavas, bananas and oranges, all sliced up—served on broad green leaves and eaten with the help of a little stick like a toothpick. It had an unusual and exciting flavour.

'You like it?' asked the boy.

'I think so,' I said.

'Don't think so,' he said. 'Just like it.'

'Is it—is it bad for the stomach?'

'For unfamiliar stomachs. So the best way to make your stomach familiar is to keep eating.'

He ordered more, in spite of my protests. Then he said, 'May I know your name?'

'Laurie,' I said, and asked him his.

'Anil, Anil Kumar! Kumar means prince, but of course I am not a prince.'

His black hair was thick and strong. His eyes were a deep brown. He wore a thin, almost transparent cotton shirt, broad white pyjamas, and open slippers with leather straps.

We ate chaat and talked, and that is how Anil and I became friends.

We would often meet in the evenings and eat at different places; and, it was as Anil said, my stomach soon became accustomed to unfamiliar cooking. We took walks across the Maidan, a spacious, grassy ground always crowded with children and dogs and cows and people making speeches. And on holidays we would cycle out of town, into the fields, down to the river.

As Holi neared, Anil began to make his preparations. He fashioned a sort of bicycle pump from a piece of bamboo, and tried it out with water. It worked!

'You'd better get out your worst clothes,' he said. 'The colour won't come off easily.'

'You don't expect me to play?' I said.

'And why not?'

'Well, first there are my parents . . .'

'And second there is yourself. You are ashamed to play.'

'No, it's not that,' I said.

Anil put his hand on my shoulder and gave me a stern look. 'Have you forgotten that a few days after we met I sent you a Christmas card?'

'That's true,' I said. 'But you sent it in February.'

'Well, I hadn't met you in December. Do you know that I pinched my father's best greeting card, and cut out the page that had been written on, in order to send it to you?'

'Yes, I noticed that. Did you want me to think you'd bought it yourself?'

'Well, they are not available in February! Anyway, the point is, I share your festivals but you do not share mine!'

And having banished all argument, he returned to fashioning his bamboo pump.

I heard the shouting and clapping, the singing and beating of drums. I jumped out of bed and ran to the window.

A procession of boys and girls were moving down the road. They were laughing and throwing colour about, and their clothes were rich shades of orange and mauve and red and green. Down the road came the procession, and down the road came Anil with his bicycle pump.

The procession passed on, but Anil lingered near our gate. It was difficult to recognize him, he wore only a loincloth and looked like an effigy of a green god.

My room had its own entrance, and I slipped out through the garden, climbed the wall, and joined Anil on the road.

Anil smiled, a white smile in a green face, and

covered my face with purple powder. Then he squirted me with his bicycle pump. He had brought a pump for me, too.

We joined the procession and went all over the town, shouting and singing and throwing colour, through the bazaar and across the Maidan, painting the town with the colours of spring.

And when I returned home in the afternoon, drenched with colour from head to foot, I found my parents waiting for me in the veranda. They didn't recognize me at first, but when they did, my father burst into laughter, while my mother told me to get under the shower immediately.

'Well, I suppose he can look after himself now,' I heard my father saying. 'We'll be here till the end of the year, and it's time he found friends of his own age.'

The Coming of Kamal

My parents had given me a small room perched on top of the bungalow, and I was sitting on my bed one morning, watching a cheeky myna hopping about on the window sill, when somebody shouted up to me from below.

'Does anyone live up there?'

'No,' I shouted back, 'nobody lives up here!'

There was a moment's silence.

'Then can I come up?' asked the person below.

'What do you want to come up for?' I said.

'To see the voice that belongs to nobody!'

'All right, come on,' I said. 'I wouldn't mind seeing what you are, either.'

'Do I just walk up the steps?'

'That's right. There are twenty-one steps. After that, turn right and you will be facing the door of my room. Twenty-one steps, remember. If you take twenty-two, you will fall off the roof.'

I heard him coming up. The myna flew off the window sill and settled in the mango tree. A warm wind came through the garden, and the leaves moved restlessly.

A boy stood in the doorway, smiling at me. He was a little taller than Anil, but thinner. He wore a red sports shirt, khaki shorts, and strong Peshawari sandals. A tray hung from his shoulders, filled with an assortment of goods.

'Here I am,' he said. 'Anil sent me.'

'Anil is out of town for a week,' I said.

'I know. He told me before he left.'

He looked about the room, at my cricket bat and books; then he looked through the opposite door, which opened out on the roof.

'Is it your roof?' he asked.

'The house is my father's,' I said. 'But the roof is mine.'

He stood at the door of the roof and looked out over the trees and the tops of houses, at the circle of blue mountains rising from the edge of the forest.

'If the roof is yours, the world is yours,' he said. 'Nobody can prove it isn't.'

He turned to me and came back to business.

'Would you like to buy something?'

In his tray were combs, buttons, reels of thread, shoelaces and cheap perfumes. I felt I had to buy something, now that he'd come all the way up my twenty-one steps. I didn't really need a comb, but I bought one for ten paisa.

'You need buttons,' he said.

'No. I don't,' I replied.

'The top button of your shirt is missing,' he observed.

'I never button my shirt at the neck, so it doesn't matter.'

'That's different,' he said, and looked me over for further signs of wear and tear. 'You'd better buy a pair of shoelaces.'

'I've got laces,' I said, making sure they were in my shoes.

He bent down to look at the laces, took one between his fingers, and snapped it in two.

'Very poor quality,' he said. 'See how easily it breaks!'

'Well, just for that I'm not going to buy any,' I said.

He sighed, shrugged, and moved towards the

door. 'You buy a comb, which you do not need. But you will not buy buttons and laces, which you do need.'

He walked slowly downstairs, and I stood in the doorway, watching him go. I was a little sorry that he was leaving; with Anil away, I did not have much company.

'What's your name?' I called out after him.

'Kamal,' he replied.

'Well, come again,' I said.

He smiled and nodded and disappeared round the side of the house.

In the evening I could see the bazaar lights from the roof and hear the jingle of tonga bells. It was becoming hotter day by day, and in the evenings everyone in town went for a walk to enjoy the breeze.

I found it difficult to walk fast on the bazaar road; besides the large number of pedestrians, there were cyclists and handcarts making movement difficult. At a little tea shop, film music was being played over a loudspeaker, adding to the noise and confusion. The balloon man was having a trying time. He was surrounded by a swarm of children who were more anxious to burst his balloons than to buy any. One or two broke away from the bunch, and went sailing over the heads of the crowd to burst over a fire in the chaat shop.

Near the clock tower the road widened and became less congested. There was a street lamp at the corner. A boy was sitting on the pavement beneath the lamp, bent over a book, absorbed in study. The noise from the road did not appear to disturb him. When I came nearer, I noticed that the boy was Kamal. The book he was reading was *David Copperfield* abridged, it was probably part of his English course.

I couldn't make up my mind whether or not to stop and talk with Kamal or carry on without disturbing him. I felt I should have spoken to him, and yet, I didn't . . .

When I had gone some way down the road I felt ashamed at not having at least greeted him, and turned around and walked back. But when I reached the lamp post, Kamal had gone.

When he came again he did not call out from below, but came straight upstairs. He examined my shirt and my shoes, and discovered that one of my shoes was still done up with only half a lace.

Triumphantly, he dropped a pair of shoelaces on the bed.

'I can't pay for them now,' I said.

'You can pay me later.'

'I don't get much pocket money, you know.'

'But surely your father will pay for shoelaces,' he said.

He had me there. Pocket money was of course meant only for sweet shops and bicycle hire and the Laurel and Hardy reissues that came to town every month.

'You go to school too?' I asked, remembering the evening when I had seen him studying beneath a lamp post.

'Yes, night school,' he said. 'I am taking my matriculation examination at the end of the month. If I pass . . .'

I could see he was thinking of the things he might be able to do if he passed. He could study for a degree, become a doctor or an engineer or a lawyer—he'd make a good lawyer, I thought—and there would be no more selling buttons and combs at street corners.

'Have you no parents?' I asked.

'They died when I was very small,' he said. 'That

was when the country was divided, and we had to leave our homes in the Punjab. I think they were killed, but I did not see it happen. I was lost in the crowd at the railway station.'

'Do you remember them well?'

'A little. My father was a farmer. He was a strict man and spoke only when it was necessary. My mother was kind, and would give me what I liked, and would sing to me in the evenings. When I lost them, I was looked after in the refugee camp. The people in charge were going to send me to a children's home, but I ran away from the camp. Soon I was making my own living. I like to be on my own, I am happier that way.'

'Where do you sleep?'

'Anywhere. On somebody's veranda, or in the Maidan, it doesn't matter in the hot weather. In winter, people are kind and give me places to sleep.'

'You can stay here whenever you like,' I said. 'I'm sure my people won't mind.'

'Thank you,' he said. 'I will come one day.'

He looked out across the roof. 'Don't you feel lonely up here? It is so quiet. I like to be near people, where there is talking and laughter.'

'So do I, sometimes. But I like to be alone, too.

I'm going to be a writer. I suppose I won't make much money, but if I like writing and if I have a few good friends, I should be happy.'

One day I accompanied him on his rounds. We met as he came out of an old house. There were two marigolds on his tray.

'An old lady lives here,' he said. 'Some say she is really a Maharani, but she is very poor now, and the house is falling to pieces. But she always buys something from me. And when I leave, she gives me one or two flowers from her garden.'

At another house, a little further down the road, Kamal was met by a girl of his own age, who chatted with him and went through his tray without buying anything. She had a round, fresh face, long black hair and wasn't wearing any shoes. Kamal gave her the two marigolds, and she took them and ran indoors.

'She never buys anything,' said Kamal, 'but she likes to talk to me. Once I gave her a ribbon, but her mother made her pay for it.'

One morning, when I opened the door of my room, I found Kamal asleep at the top of the steps. His tray lay to one side.

I shook him gently and he woke immediately,

blinking in the sharp, early morning sunshine.

'Why didn't you come in?' I asked. 'Why didn't you wake me up?'

'It was late, Laurie. I didn't want to disturb you.'

'Somebody could have stolen your things.'

'Oh, nobody has ever stolen anything from me.'

He stayed in my room that night, and we sat up till past midnight, talking of different things. I told him of Jersey, the island where I had spent much of my youth, of London, where I had often gone with my parents, and of my voyage out to India by way of the Suez Canal. He, in turn, told me about his village in the Punjab, and of his hopes and ambitions.

The exams came at last, and for a week Kamal put aside his tray of merchandize and spent his time at the examination centre. He was quite confident that he had done his papers well, and when it was all over, he took up his tray and went on his rounds again.

On the day the results were expected, I rose early and walked to the news agency. Anil was there too, buying vegetables for his mother. We bought a paper and looked down the columns concerning our district but we couldn't find Kamal's number in the list of successful candidates.

We were very disappointed. When I returned to my room, I found Kamal sitting on the steps. I didn't have to tell him the news. He knew already. I sat down beside him, and we were silent for some time.

'If only you'd had more time to study,' I said.

'I'll have plenty of time now,' he said. 'Another year. That means you and Anil and I will finish school together. Then we'll celebrate!'

He got to his feet with his tray hanging from his shoulders.

'What would you like to buy?' he said.

I took another comb from his tray and put it in my pocket. I needed soap and buttons but I took a comb, which I didn't need. There was more fun in doing that.

The Pool

It was going to rain. I could see the rain moving across the foothills, and I could smell it in the breeze. But instead of turning homewards, I pushed my way through the leaves and brambles that grew across the forest path. I had heard the sound of running water at the bottom of the hill, and I was determined to find this hidden stream.

I had to slide down a rock face into a small ravine, and there I found the stream running over a bed of shingle. I removed my shoes and started walking upstream. A large glossy black bird with a curved red beak hooted at me as I passed and a paradise flycatcher—this one I couldn't fail to recognize, with its long fan-like tail beating the air— swooped across the stream. Water trickled down from the hillside, from amongst ferns and grasses and wild flowers; and the hills, rising steeply on either side, kept the ravine in shadow. The rocks were smooth, almost soft, and some of them were grey and some yellow. A small waterfall came down the rocks and formed a deep round pool of apple-green water.

When I saw the pool, I turned and ran home. I wanted to tell Anil and Kamal about it. It began to rain, but I didn't stop to take shelter, I ran all the way home—through the sal forest, across the dry river-bed, through the outskirts of the town.

Though Anil usually chose the adventures we were to have, the pool was my own discovery, and I was proud of it.

'We'll call it Laurie's Pool,' said Kamal. 'And remember, it's a secret pool. No one else must know of it.'

I think it was the pool that brought us together more than anything else.

Kamal was the best swimmer. He dived off rocks and went gliding about under the water like a long golden fish. Anil had strong legs and arms, and he threshed about with much vigour but little skill. I could dive off a rock too, but I usually landed on my stomach.

There were slim silver fish in the stream. At first, we tried catching them with a line, but they soon learnt the art of taking the bait without being caught on the hook. Next, we tried a bedsheet (Anil had removed it from his mother's laundry) which we stretched across one end of the stream; but the fish wouldn't come anywhere near it. Eventually Anil, without telling us, procured a stick of gunpowder. And Kamal and I were startled out of an afternoon siesta by a flash across the water and a deafening explosion. Half the hillside tumbled into the pool, and Anil along with it. We got him out, along with a large supply of stunned fish which were too small for eating. Anil, however, didn't want all his work to go waste; so he roasted the fish over a fire and ate them himself.

The effects of the explosion gave Anil another idea, which was to enlarge our pool by building a dam across one end. This he accomplished with our combined labour. But he had chosen a week when there had been heavy rain in the hills, and we had barely finished the dam when a torrent of water came rushing down the bed of the stream, bursting our earthworks and flooding the ravine. Our clothes were carried away by the current, and we had to wait until it was night before creeping into town through the darkest alleyways. Anil was spotted at a street corner, but he posed as a naked sadhu and began calling for alms, and finally slipped in through the back door of his house without being recognized. I had to lend Kamal some of my clothes, and these, being on the small side, made him look odd and gangly.

Our other activities at the pool included wrestling and buffalo riding.

We wrestled on a strip of sand that ran beside the stream. Anil had often attended wrestling akharas and was something of an expert. Kamal and I usually combined against him and after five or ten minutes of furious, unscientific struggle, we usually succeeded in flattening Anil into the sand; Kamal would sit on his head, and I would sit on his legs until he admitted defeat. There was no fun in taking him on singly, because he knew too many tricks for us.

We rode on a couple of buffaloes that sometimes came to drink and wallow in the more muddy parts of the stream. Buffaloes are fine, sluggish creatures, always in search of a soft, slushy resting place. We would climb on their backs, kick, yell and urge them forward, but on no occasion did we succeed in getting them to carry us anywhere. If they got tired of our antics, they would merely roll over on their backs, taking us with them into a bed of muddy water.

Not that it mattered how muddy we got, because we had only to dive into the pool to get rid of it all. The buffaloes couldn't get to the pool because of its narrow outlet and the slippery rocks.

If it was possible for Anil and me to leave our homes at night, we would come to the pool for a swim by moonlight. We would often find Kamal there before us. He wasn't afraid of the dark or the surrounding forest, where there were panthers and jungle cats. We bathed silently at nights, because the stillness of the surrounding jungle seemed to discourage high spirits; but sometimes Kamal would sing—he had a clear, ringing voice—and we would float the red, long-fingered poinsettias downstream.

The pool was to be our principal meeting place during the coming months. It was not that we couldn't meet in town. But the pool was secret, known only to us, and it gave us a feeling of conspiracy and adventure to meet there after school. It was at the pool that we made our plans, it was at the pool that we first spoke of the glacier; but several weeks and a few other exploits were to pass before that particular dream materialized.

Ghosts on the Veranda

Anil's mother's memory was stored with an incredible amount of folklore, and she would sometimes astonish us with her stories of sprites and mischievous ghosts.

One evening, when Anil's father was out of town, and Kamal and I had been invited to stay the night at Anil's upper-storey flat in the bazaar, his mother began to tell us about the various types of ghosts she had known. Just then, Mulia, the servant, having taken a bath, came out to the veranda, with her hair loose.

'My girl, you ought not to leave your hair loose like that,' said Anil's mother. 'It is better to tie a knot in it.'

'But I have not oiled it yet,' said Mulia.

'Never mind, but you should not leave your hair

loose towards sunset. There are spirits called jinns who are attracted by long hair and pretty black eyes like yours. They may be tempted to carry you away!'

'How dreadful!' exclaimed Mulia, hurriedly tying a knot in her hair, and going indoors to be on the safe side.

Kamal, Anil and I sat on a string cot, facing Anil's mother, who sat on another cot. She was not much older than thirty-two, and had often been mistaken for Anil's elder sister; she came from a village near Mathura, a part of the country famous for its gods, spirits and demons.

'Can you see jinns, aunty-ji?' I asked.

'Sometimes,' she said. 'There was an Urdu teacher in Mathura, whose pupils were about the same age as you. One of the boys was very good at his lessons. One day, while he sat at his desk in a corner of the classroom, the teacher asked him to fetch a book from the cupboard which stood at the far end of the room. The boy, who felt lazy that morning, didn't move from his seat. He merely stretched out his hand, took the book from the cupboard, and handed it to the teacher. Everyone was astonished, because the boy's arm had

stretched about four yards before touching the book! They realized that he was a jinn. It was the reason for his being so good at games and exercises which required great agility.'

'Well, I wish I were a jinn,' said Anil. 'Especially for volleyball matches.'

Anil's mother then told us about the munjia, a mischievous ghost who lives in lonely peepal trees. When a munjia is annoyed, he rushes out from his tree and upsets tongas, bullock-carts and cycles. Even a bus is known to have been upset by a munjia.

'If you are passing beneath a peepal tree at night,' warned Anil's mother, 'be careful not to yawn without covering your mouth or snapping your fingers in front of it. If you don't remember to do that, the munjia will jump down your throat and completely ruin your digestion!'

In an attempt to change the subject, Kamal mentioned that a friend of his had found a snake in his bed one morning.

'Did he kill it?' asked Anil's mother anxiously.

'No, it slipped away,' said Kamal.

'Good,' she said. 'It is lucky if you see a snake early in the morning.'

'But what if the snake bites you?' I asked.

'It won't bite you if you let it alone,' she said.

By eleven o'clock, after we had finished our dinner and heard a few more ghost stories—including one about Anil's grandmother, whose spirit paid the family a visit—Kamal and I were most reluctant to leave the company on the veranda and retire to the room which had been set apart for us. It did not make us feel any better to be told by Anil's mother that we should recite certain magical verses to keep away the more mischievous spirits. We tried one, which went—

Bhoot, pret, pisach, dana
Choo mantar, sab nikal jana,
Mano, mano, Shiv ka kahna

which, roughly translated, means—

Ghosts, spirits, goblins, sprites,
Away you fly, don't come tonight,
Or with great Shiva you'll have to fight!

Shiva, the Destroyer, is one of the three major Hindu deities.

But the more we repeated the verse, the more uneasy we became, and when I got into bed (after carefully examining it for snakes), I couldn't lie still, but kept twisting and turning and looking at the walls for moving shadows. Kamal attempted to raise our spirits by singing softly, but this only made the atmosphere more eerie. After a while we heard someone knocking at the door, and the voices of Anil and the servant girl, Mulia. Getting up and opening the door, I found them looking pale and anxious. They, too, had succeeded in frightening themselves as a result of Anil's mother's stories.

'Are you all right?' asked Anil. 'Wouldn't you like to sleep in our part of the house? It might be safer. Mulia will help us to carry the beds across!'

'We're quite all right,' protested Kamal and I, refusing to admit we were nervous; but we were hustled along to the other side of the flat as though a band of ghosts was conspiring against us. Anil's mother had been absent during all this activity, but suddenly we heard her screaming from the direction of the room we had just left.

'Laurie and Kamal have disappeared!' she cried. 'Their beds have gone, too!'

And then, when she came out to the veranda

and saw us dashing about in our pyjamas, she gave another scream and collapsed on a cot.

After that, we didn't allow Anil's mother to tell us ghost stories at night.

The Big Race

I was awakened by the sound of a hornbill honking in the banyan tree. I lay in bed, looking through the open window as the early morning sunshine crept up the wall. I knew it was a holiday, and that there was something important to be done that day, but for some time I couldn't quite remember what it was. Then, as the room got brighter, and the hornbill stopped his noise, I remembered.

It was the day of the big race.

I leapt out of bed, pulled open a dressing-table drawer and brought out a cardboard box punctured with little holes. I opened the lid to see if Maharani was all right.

Maharani, my bamboo-beetle, was asleep on the core of an apple. I had given her a week's rigorous training for the monsoon beetle race, and she was enjoying a well-earned rest before the big event. I did not disturb her.

Closing the box, I crept out of the house by the back door. I did not want my parents to see me sneaking off to the municipal park at that early hour.

When I reached the gardens, the early morning sun was just beginning to make emeralds of the dewdrops, and the grass was cool and springy to my bare feet. A group of boys had gathered in a corner of the gardens, and among them were Kamal and Anil.

Anil's black rhino-beetle was the favourite. It was a big beetle, with an aggressive forehead rather like its owner's. It was called Black Prince. Kamal's beetle was quite ordinary in size, but it possessed a long pair of whiskers (I suspected it belonged to the cockroach rather than the beetle family), and was called Moochha, which is Hindi for moustache.

There were one or two other entries, but none of them looked promising and interest centred on Black Prince, Moochha, and my own Maharani who was still asleep on her apple core. A few bets were being made, in coins or marbles, and a prize for the winner was on display; a great stag-beetle, quite dangerous to look at, which would enable the winner to start a stable and breed beetles on a large scale.

There was some confusion when Kamal's Moochha escaped from his box and took a preliminary canter over the grass, but he was soon caught and returned to his paddock. Moochha appeared to be in good form, and several boys put their marbles on him.

The course was about six feet long, the tracks six inches wide. The tracks were fenced with strips of cardboard so that the contestants would not move over to each other's path or leave the course altogether. They could only go forwards or backwards. They were held at the starting point by another piece of cardboard, which would be placed behind them as soon as the race began.

A little Sikh boy in a yellow pyjama suit was acting as starter, and he kept blowing his whistle for order and attention. Eventually he gained enough silence in which to announce the rules of the race: the contesting beetles were not allowed to be touched during the race, or blown at from behind, or bribed forward with bits of food. Only moral assistance was allowed, in the form of cheering and advice.

Moochha and Black Prince were already at the starting point, but Maharani seemed unwilling to leave her apple core, and I had to drag her to the starting post. There was further delay when Moochha got his whiskers entangled in the legs of a rival, but they were soon separated and the beetles placed in separate lanes. The race was about to start.

Kamal sat on his haunches, very quiet and serious, looking from Moochha to the finishing line and back again. I was biting my nails. Anil's bushy eyebrows were bunched together in a scowl. There was a tense hush amongst the spectators.

'Pee-ee-eep!' went the whistle.

And they were off!

Or rather, Moochha and Black Prince were off because Maharani was still at the starting post, wondering what had happened to her apple core.

Everyone was cheering madly, Anil was jumping about, and Kamal was shouting himself hoarse.

Moochha was going at a spanking rate. Black Prince really wasn't taking much interest in the proceedings, but at least he was moving, and everything could happen in a race of this nature. I was in a furious temper. All the coaching I had

given Maharani appeared to be of no use. She was still looking confused and a little resentful at having been deprived of her apple.

Then Moochha suddenly stopped, about two feet from the finishing line. He seemed to be having trouble with his whiskers, and kept twitching them this way and that. Black Prince was catching up inch by inch, and both Anil and Kamal were hopping about with excitement. Nobody was paying any attention to Maharani, who was looking suspiciously at the other beetles in the rear. No doubt she suspected them of having something to do with the disappearance of her apple. I begged her to make an effort. It was with difficulty that I prevented myself from giving her a push, but that would have meant disqualification.

As Black Prince drew level with Moochha, he stopped and appeared to be enquiring about his rival's whiskers. Anil and Kamal now became even more frantic in their efforts to encourage their racers, and the cheering on all sides was deafening.

Maharani, enraged at having been deprived of her apple core, now decided to make a bid for liberty and rushed forward in great style.

I gave a cry of joy, but the others did not notice

this new challenge until Maharani had drawn level with her rivals. There was a gasp of surprise from the spectators, and Maharani dashed across the finishing line in record time.

Everyone cheered the gallant outsider. Anil and Kamal very sportingly shook my hand and congratulated me on my methods. Coins and marbles passed from hand to hand. The little Sikh boy blew his whistle for silence and presented me with the first prize.

I examined the new beetle with respect and gently stroked its hard, smooth back. Then in case Maharani should feel jealous, I put away the prize beetle and returned Maharani to her apple core. I was determined that I would not indulge in any favouritism.

To the Hills

At the end of August, when the rains were nearly over, we met at the pool to make plans for the autumn holidays. We had bathed and were stretched out in the shade of the fresh, rain-washed sal trees, when Kamal, pointing vaguely to the distant mountains, said: 'Why don't we go to the Pindari Glacier?'

'The glacier!' exclaimed Anil. 'But that's all snow and ice!'

'Of course it is,' said Kamal. 'But there's a path through the mountains that goes all the way to the foot of the glacier. It's only fifty-four miles.'

'Only fifty-four miles! Do you mean we must— *walk* fifty-four miles?'

'Well, there's no other way,' said Kamal. 'Unless you prefer to sit on a mule. But your legs are too long, they'll be trailing along the ground. No, we'll have to walk. It will take us about ten days to get to the glacier and back, but if we take enough food there'll be no problem. There are dak bungalows to stay in at night.'

'Kamal gets all the best ideas,' I said. 'But I suppose Anil and I will have to get our parents' permission. And some money.'

'My mother won't let me go,' said Anil. 'She says the mountains are full of ghosts. And she thinks I'll get up to some mischief. How can one get up to mischief on a lonely mountain? Have you been on the mountains, Laurie?'

'I've been on English mountains,' I said, 'but they're not half as high as these. Kamal seems to know about them.'

'Only what I've read in books,' said Kamal. 'I'm sure it won't be dangerous, people are always going to the glacier. Can you see that peak above the others on the right?' He pointed to the distant snow range, barely visible against the soft blue sky. 'The Pindari Glacier is below it. It's at 12,000 feet, I think, but we won't need any special equipment. There'll be snow only for the final two or three miles. Do you know that it's the beginning of the river Sarayu?'

'You mean our river?' asked Anil, thinking of the little river that wandered along the outskirts of the town, joining the Ganges further downstream.

'Yes. But it's only a trickle where it starts.'

'How much money will we need?' I asked, determined to be practical.

'Well. I've saved twenty rupees,' said Kamal.

'But won't you need that for your books?' I asked.

'No, this is extra. If each of us brings twenty rupees, we should have enough. There's nothing to spend money on, once we are up on the mountains. There are only one or two villages on the way and food is scarce, so we'll have to take plenty of food with us. I learnt all this from the Tourist Office.'

'Kamal's been planning this without our knowledge,' complained Anil.

'He always plans in advance,' I said. 'But it's a good idea, and it should be a fine adventure.'

'All right,' said Anil. 'But Laurie will have to be with me when I ask my mother. She thinks Laurie is very sensible, and might let me go if he says it's quite safe.' And he ended the discussion by jumping into the pool, where we soon joined him.

Though my mother hesitated about letting me

go, my father said it was a wonderful idea and was only sorry because he couldn't accompany us himself (which was a relief, as we didn't want our parents along); and though Anil's father hesitated— or rather, because he hesitated—his mother said yes, of course Anil must go, the mountain air would be good for his health. A puzzling remark, because Anil's health had never been better. The bazaar people, when they heard that Anil might be away for a couple of weeks, were overjoyed at the prospect of a quiet spell, and pressed his father to let him go.

On a cloudy day, promising rain, we bundled ourselves into the bus that was to take us to Kapkote (where people lose their caps and coats, punned Anil), the starting point of our trek. Each of us carried a haversack, and we had also brought along a good-sized bedding roll which, apart from blankets, also contained rice and flour thoughtfully provided by Anil's mother. We had no idea how we would carry the bedding roll once we started walking. But we didn't worry much over minor details: an astrologer had told Anil's mother it was a good day for travelling, so we decided all would be well.

We were soon in the hills, on a winding road

that took us up and up, until we saw the valley and our town spread out beneath us, the river a silver ribbon across the plain. Kamal pointed to a patch of dense sal forest and said, 'Our pool must be there!' We took a sharp bend, and the valley disappeared, and the mountains towered above us.

We had dull headaches by the time we reached Kapkote, but when we got down from the bus a cool breeze freshened us. At the wayside shop we drank glasses of hot, sweet tea, and the shopkeeper told us we could spend the night in one of his rooms. It was pleasant at Kapkote, the hills wooded with deodar trees, the lower slopes planted with fresh green paddy. At night, there was a wind moaning in the trees and it found its way through the cracks in the windows and eventually through our blankets. Then, right outside the door, a dog began howling at the moon. It had been a good day for travelling, but the astrologer hadn't warned us that it would be a bad night for sleep.

Next morning, we washed our faces at a small stream about a hundred yards from the shop and filled our water bottles for the day's march. A boy from the nearby village sat on a rock, studying our movements.

'Where are you going?' he asked, unable to suppress his curiosity.

'To the glacier,' said Kamal.

'Let me come with you,' said the boy. 'I know the way.'

'You're too small,' said Anil. 'We need someone who can carry our bedding roll.'

'I'm small,' said the boy, 'but I'm strong. I'm not a weakling like the boys in the plains.' Though he was shorter than any of us, he certainly looked sturdy, and had a muscular well-knit body and pink cheeks. 'See!' he said, and picking up a rock the size of a football, he heaved it across the stream.

'I think he can come with us,' I said.

And the boy, whose name was Bisnu, dashed off to inform his people of his employment—we had agreed to pay him a rupee a day for acting as our guide and 'sherpa'.

And then we started walking, at first, above the little Sarayu river, then climbing higher along the rough mule track, always within sound of the water. Kamal wanted to bathe in the river. I said it was too far, and Anil said we wouldn't reach the dak bungalow before dark if we went for a swim. Regretfully, we left the river behind, and marched on through a forest of oaks, over wet, rotting leaves that made a soft carpet for our feet. We ate at noon, under an oak. As we didn't want to waste any time making a fire—not on this first crucial day—we ate beans from a tin and drank most of our water.

In the afternoon we came to the river again. The water was swifter now, green and bubbling still far below us. We saw two boys in the water, swimming in an inlet which reminded us of our own secret pool. They waved, and invited us to join them. We returned their greeting but it would have taken us an hour to get down to the river and up again; so we continued on our way.

We walked fifteen miles on that first day—our speed was to decrease after this and we were at the dak bungalow by six o'clock. Bisnu busied himself collecting sticks for a fire. Anil found the bungalow's watchman asleep in a patch of fading sunlight and roused him. The watchman, who hadn't been bothered by visitors for weeks, grumbled at our intrusion, but opened a room for us. He also produced some potatoes from his quarters, and these we roasted for dinner.

It became cold after the sun had gone down and we remained close to Bisnu's fire. The damp sticks burnt fitfully. By this time Bisnu had fully justified his inclusion in our party. He had balanced the bedding roll on his shoulders as though it were full of cotton wool instead of blankets. Now he was helping with the cooking. And we were glad to have him sharing our hot potatoes and strong tea.

There were only two beds in the room and we pushed these together, apportioning out the blankets as fairly as possible. Then the four of us leapt into bed, shivering in the cold. We were already over 5000 feet. Bisnu, in his own peculiar way, had wrapped a scarf round his neck, though a cotton singlet and shorts were all that he wore for the night.

'Tell us a story, Laurie,' said Anil. 'It will help us to fall asleep.'

I told them one of his mother's stories, about a boy and a girl who had been changed into a pair of buffaloes and then Bisnu told us about the ghost of a sadhu, who was to be seen sitting in the snow by moonlight, not far from the glacier. Far from putting us to sleep, this story kept us awake for hours.

'Aren't you asleep yet?' I asked Anil in the middle of the night.

'No, you keep kicking me,' he lied.

'We don't have enough blankets,' complained Kamal. 'It's too cold to sleep.'

'I never sleep till it's very late,' mumbled Bisnu from the bottom of the bed.

No one was prepared to admit that our imaginations were keeping us awake.

After a little while we heard a thud on the corrugated tin sheets, and then the sound of someone—or something—scrambling about on the roof. Anil, Kamal and I sat up in bed, startled out of our wits. Bisnu, who had won the race to be the first one to fall asleep, merely turned over on his side and grunted.

'It's only a bear,' he said. 'Didn't you notice the pumpkins on the roof? Bears love pumpkins.'

For half an hour we had to listen to the bear as it clambered about on the roof, feasting on the watchman's ripening pumpkins. Finally, there was silence. Kamal and I crawled out of our blankets and went to the window. And through the frosted glass we saw a black Himalayan bear ambling across the slope in front of the bungalow, a fat pumpkin held between its paws.

To the River

It was raining when we woke and the mountains were obscured by a heavy mist. We delayed our departure, playing football on the veranda with one of the pumpkins that had fallen off the roof. At noon the rain stopped and the sun shone through the clouds. As the mist lifted, we saw the snow range, the great peaks of Nanda Kot and Trishul stepping into the sky.

'It's different up here,' said Kamal. 'I feel a different person.'

'That's the altitude,' I said. 'As we go higher, we'll get lighter in the head.'

'Anil is light in the head already,' said Kamal. 'I hope the altitude isn't too much for him.'

'If you two are going to be witty,' said Anil, 'I shall go off with Bisnu, and you'll have to find the way yourselves.'

Bisnu grinned at each of us in turn to show us that he wasn't taking sides, and after a breakfast of boiled eggs, we set off on our trek to the next bungalow.

Rain had made the ground slippery and we were soon ankle-deep in slush. Our next bungalow lay in a narrow valley, on the banks of the rushing Pindar river, which twisted its way through the mountains. We were not sure how far we had to go, but nobody seemed to be in a hurry. On an impulse, I decided to hurry on ahead of the others. I wanted to be waiting for them at the river.

The path dropped steeply, then rose and went round a big mountain. I met a woodcutter and asked him how far it was to the river. He was a short, stocky man, with gnarled hands and a weathered face.

'Seven miles,' he said. 'Are you alone?'

'No, the others are following but I cannot wait for them. If you meet them, tell them I'll be waiting at the river.'

The path descended steeply now, and I had to run a little. It was a dizzy, winding path. The hillside was covered with lush green ferns and, in the trees, unseen birds sang loudly. Soon I was in the valley and the path straightened out.

A girl was coming from the opposite direction. She held a long, curved knife, with which she had been cutting grass and fodder. There were rings in her nose and ears and her arms were covered with heavy bangles. The bangles made music when she moved her hands: it was as though her hands spoke a language of their own.

'How far is it to the river?' I asked.

The girl had probably never been near the river, or she may have been thinking of another one, because she replied, 'Twenty miles,' without any hesitation.

I laughed and ran down the path. A parrot screeched suddenly, flew low over my head—a flash of blue and green—and took the course of the path, while I followed its dipping flight, until the path rose and the bird disappeared into the trees.

A trickle of water came from the hillside and I stopped to drink. The water was cold and sharp and very refreshing. I had walked alone for nearly an hour. Presently, I saw a boy ahead of me, driving a few goats along the path.

'How far is it to the river?' I asked, when I caught up with him.

The boy said, 'Oh, not far, just round the next hill.'

As I was hungry, I produced some dry bread from my pocket and, breaking it in two, offered half to the boy. We sat on the grassy hillside and ate in silence. Then we walked on together and began talking; and talking, I did not notice the smarting of my feet and the distance I had covered. But after some time the boy had to diverge along another path, and I was once more on my own.

I missed the village boy. I looked up and down the path, but I could see no one, no sign of Anil and Kamal and Bisnu, and the river was not in sight either. I began to feel discouraged. But I couldn't turn back; I was determined to be at the river before the others.

And so I walked on, along the muddy path, past terraced fields and small stone houses, until there were no more fields and houses, only forest and sun and silence.

The silence was impressive and a little frightening. It was different from the silence of a room or an empty street. Nor was there any movement, except for the bending of grass beneath my feet and the circling of a hawk high above the fir trees.

And then, as I rounded a sharp bend, the silence broke into sound.

The sound of the river.

Far down in the valley, the river tumbled over itself in its impatience to reach the plains. I began to run, slipped and stumbled, but continued running.

And the water was blue and white and wonderful.

When Anil, Kamal and Bisnu arrived, the four of us bravely decided to bathe in the little river. The late afternoon sun was still warm, but the water— so clear and inviting—proved to be ice-cold. Only twenty miles upstream the river emerged as a little trickle from the glacier and, in its swift descent down the mountain slopes, did not give the sun a chance to penetrate its waters. But we were determined to bathe, to wash away the dust and sweat of our two days' trudging, and we leapt about in the shallows like startled porpoises, slapping water on each other and gasping with the shock of each immersion. Bisnu, more accustomed to mountain streams than ourselves, ventured across in an attempt to catch an otter, but wasn't fast enough. Then we were on the springy grass, wrestling each other in order to get warm.

The bungalow stood on a ledge just above the river, and the sound of the water rushing down the mountain defile could be heard at all times. The sound of the birds, which we had grown used to, was drowned by the sound of the water, but the birds themselves could be seen, many-coloured, standing out splendidly against the dark green forest foliage: the red-crowned jay, the paradise flycatcher, the purple whistling-thrush and others that we could not recognize.

Higher up the mountain, above some terraced land where oats and barley were grown, stood a small cluster of huts. This, we were told by the watchman, was the last village on the way to the glacier. It was, in fact, one of the last villages in India, because if we crossed the difficult passes beyond the glacier, we would find ourselves in Tibet. We told the watchman we would be quite satisfied if we reached the glacier.

Then Anil made the mistake of mentioning the Abominable Snowman, of whom we had been reading in the papers. The people of Nepal believe in the existence of the Snowman, and our watchman was a Nepali.

'Yes, I have seen the Yeti,' he told us. 'A great shaggy flat-footed creature. In winter, when it snows heavily, he passes by the bungalow at night. I have seen his tracks the next morning.'

'Does he come this way in summer?' I asked anxiously. We were sitting before another of Bisnu's fires, drinking tea with condensed milk, and trying to get through a black, sticky sweet which the watchman had produced from his tin trunk.

'The Yeti doesn't come here in summer,' said the old man. 'But I have seen the Lidini sometimes. You have to be careful of her.'

'What is a Lidini?' asked Kamal.

'Ah!' said the watchman mysteriously. 'You have heard of the Abominable Snowman, no doubt, but there are few who have heard of the Abominable Snow-woman! And yet, she is far more dangerous of the two!'

'What is she like?' asked Anil, and we all craned forward.

'She is of the same height as the Yeti—about seven feet when her back is straight—and her hair is much longer. She has very long teeth and nails.

Her feet face inwards, but she can run very fast, especially downhill. If you see a Lidini and she chases you, always run uphill. She tires quickly because of her feet. But when running downhill she has no trouble at all, and you have to be very fast to escape her!'

'Well, we're all good runners,' said Anil with a nervous laugh. 'But it's just a fairy story, I don't believe a word of it.'

'But you *must* believe fairy stories,' I said, remembering a performance of Peter Pan in London, when those in the audience who believed in fairies were asked to clap their hands in order to save Tinker Bell's life. 'Even if they aren't true,' I added, deciding there was a world of difference between Tinker Bell and the Abominable Snow-woman.

'Well, I don't believe there's a Snowman *or* a Snow-woman!' declared Anil.

The watchman was most offended and refused to tell us anything about the Sagpa and Sagpani; but Bisnu knew about them, and later, when we were in bed, he told us that they were similar to Snowmen but much smaller. Their favourite pastime was to sleep, and they became very annoyed if anyone woke them up, and became ferocious, and did not give one much time to start running uphill. The Sagpa and Sagpani sometimes kidnapped small children and, taking them to their cave, would look after the children very carefully, feeding them on fruit, honey, rice, and earthworms.

'When the Sagpa isn't looking,' he said, 'you can throw the earthworms over your shoulder.'

The Glacier

It was a fine sunny morning when we set out to cover the last seven miles to the glacier. We had expected this to be a stiff climb, but the last dak bungalow was situated at well over 10,000 feet above sea level, and the ascent was to be fairly gradual.

And then suddenly, abruptly, there were no more trees. As the bungalow dropped out of sight, the trees and bushes gave way to short grass and little blue and pink alpine flowers. The snow peaks were close now, ringing us in on every side. We passed waterfalls, cascading hundreds of feet down precipitous rock faces, thundering into the little river. A great golden eagle hovered over us for some time.

'I feel different again,' said Kamal.

'We're very high now,' I said. 'I hope we won't get headaches.'

'I've got one already,' complained Anil. 'Let's have some tea.'

We had left our cooking utensils at the bungalow, expecting to return there for the night, and had brought with us only a few biscuits, chocolate, and a thermos of tea. We finished the tea, and Bisnu scrambled about on the grassy slopes, collecting wild strawberries. They were tiny strawberries, very sweet, and they did nothing to satisfy our appetites. There was no sign of habitation or human life. The only creatures to be found at that height were the gurals—sure-footed mountain goats—and an occasional snow leopard, or a bear.

We found and explored a small cave and then, turning a bend, came unexpectedly upon the glacier.

The hill fell away and there, confronting us, was a great white field of snow and ice, cradled between two peaks that could only have been the abode of the gods. We were speechless for several minutes. Kamal took my hand and held on to it for reassurance; perhaps he was not sure that what he saw was real. Anil's mouth hung open. Bisnu's eyes glittered with excitement.

We proceeded cautiously on the snow, supporting each other on the slippery surface, but we could not go far, because we were quite unequipped for any high-altitude climbing. It was pleasant to feel that we were the only boys in our town who had climbed so high. A few black rocks jutted out from the snow, and we sat down on them to feast our eyes on the view. The sun reflected sharply from the snow and we felt surprisingly warm.

'Let's sunbathe!' said Anil, on a sudden impulse.

'Yes, let's do that!' I said.

In a few minutes we had taken off our clothes and, sitting on the rocks, were exposing ourselves to the elements. It was delicious to feel the sun crawling over my skin. Within half an hour I was a post-box red, and so was Bisnu, and the two of us decided to get into our clothes before the sun scorched the skin off our backs. Kamal and Anil appeared to be more resilient to sunlight and laughed at our discomfiture. Bisnu and I avenged ourselves by gathering up handfuls of snow and rubbing it on their backs. They dressed quickly enough after that, Anil leaping about like a performing monkey.

Meanwhile, almost imperceptibly, clouds had

covered some of the peaks, and a white mist drifted down the mountain slopes. It was time to get back to the bungalow; we would barely make it before dark.

We had not gone far when lightning began to sizzle above the mountain tops, followed by waves of thunder.

'Let's run!' shouted Anil. 'We can take shelter in the cave!'

The clouds could hold themselves in no longer, and the rain came down suddenly, stinging our faces as it was whipped up by an icy wind. Half-blinded, we ran as fast as we could along the slippery path and stumbled, drenched and exhausted, into the little cave.

The cave was mercifully dry and not very dark. We remained at the entrance, watching the rain sweep past us, listening to the wind whistling down the long gorge.

'It will take some time to stop,' said Kamal.

'No, it will pass soon,' said Bisnu. 'These storms are short and fierce.'

Anil produced his pocket knife and, to pass the time, we carved our names in the smooth rock of the cave.

'We will come here again, when we are older,' said Kamal, 'and perhaps our names will still be here.'

It had grown dark by the time the rain stopped. A full moon helped us find our way. We went slowly and carefully. The rain had loosened the earth and stones kept rolling down the hillside. I was afraid of starting a landslide.

'I hope we don't meet the Lidini now,' said Anil fervently.

'I thought you didn't believe in her,' I said.

'I don't,' replied Anil. 'But what if I'm wrong?'

We saw only a gural, poised on the brow of a precipice, silhouetted against the sky.

And then the path vanished.

Had it not been for the bright moonlight, we might have walked straight into an empty void. The rain had caused a landslide and where there had been a narrow path there was now only a precipice of loose, slippery shale.

'We'll have to go back,' said Bisnu. 'It will be too dangerous to try and cross in the dark.'

'We'll sleep in the cave,' I suggested.

'We've nothing to sleep in,' said Anil. 'Not a single blanket between us—and nothing to eat!'

'We'll just have to rough it till morning,' said Kamal. 'It will be better than breaking our necks here.'

We returned to the cave, which did at least have the virtue of being dry. Bisnu had matches and he made a fire with some dry sticks which had been left in the cave by a previous party. We ate what was left of a loaf of bread.

There was no sleep for any of us that night. We lay close to each other for comfort, but the ground was hard and uneven. And every noise we heard outside the cave made us think of leopards and bears and even Abominable Snowmen.

We got up as soon as there was a faint glow in the sky. The snow peaks were bright pink, but we were too tired and hungry and worried to care for the beauty of the sunrise. We took the path to the landslide and once again looked for a way across. Kamal ventured to take a few steps on the loose pebbles, but the ground gave way immediately, and we had to grab him by the arms and shoulders to prevent him from sliding a hundred feet down the gorge.

'Now what are we going to do?' I asked.

'Look for another way,' said Bisnu.

'But do you know of any?'

And we all turned to look at Bisnu, expecting him to provide the solution to our problem.

'I have heard of a way,' said Bisnu, 'but I have never used it. It will be a little dangerous, I think. The path has not been used for several years—not since the traders stopped coming in from Tibet.'

'Never mind, we'll try it,' said Anil.

'We will have to cross the glacier first,' said Bisnu. 'That's the main problem.'

We looked at each other in silence. The glacier didn't look difficult to cross, but we knew that it would not be easy for novices like us. For almost a quarter of a mile it consisted of hard, slippery ice.

Anil was the first to arrive at a decision.

'Come on,' he said. 'There's no time to waste.'

We were soon on the glacier. And we remained on it for a long time. For every two steps forward, we slid one step backward. Our progress was slow and awkward. Sometimes, after advancing several yards across the ice at a steep incline, one of us would slip back and the others would have to slither down to help him up. At one particularly difficult spot, I dropped our water bottle and, grabbing at it, lost my footing, fell full-length and went sliding some twenty feet down the ice slope.

I had sprained my wrist and hurt my knee, and was to prove a liability for the rest of the trek.

Kamal tied his handkerchief round my hand, and Anil took charge of the water bottle, which we had filled with ice. Using my good hand to grab Bisnu's legs whenever I slipped, I struggled on behind the others.

It was almost noon, and we were quite famished, when we put our feet on grass again. And then we had another steep climb, clutching at roots and grasses, before we reached the path that Bisnu had spoken about. It was little more than a goat track, but it took us round the mountain and brought us within sight of the dak bungalow.

'I could eat a whole chicken,' said Kamal.

'I could eat two,' I said.

'I could eat a Snowman,' said Bisnu.

'And I could eat the chowkidar,' said Anil.

Fortunately for the chowkidar, he had anticipated our hunger, and when we staggered into the bungalow late in the afternoon, we found a meal waiting for us. True, there was no chicken, but so ravenous did we feel, that even the lowly onion tasted delicious!

We had Bisnu to thank for getting us back successfully. He had brought us over mountain and glacier with all the skill and confidence of a boy who had the Himalayas in his blood.

We took our time getting back to Kapkote, fished in the Sarayu river, bathed with the village boys we had seen on our way up, collected strawberries and ferns and wild flowers, and finally said goodbye to Bisnu.

Anil wanted to take Bisnu along with us, but the boy's parents refused to let him go, saying that he was too young for the life in a city but we were of the opinion that Bisnu could have taught the city boys a few things.

'Never mind,' said Kamal. 'We'll go on another trip next year and we'll take you with us, Bisnu. We'll write and let you know our plans.'

This promise made Bisnu happy and he saw us off at the bus stop, shouldering our bedding to the end. Then he skimmed up the trunk of a fir tree to have a better view of us leaving and we saw him waving to us from the tree as our bus went round

the bend from Kapkote, and the hills were left
behind and the plains stretched out below.

Going Away

'Well, I'm glad you enjoyed your hike,' said my father. 'It will give you something pleasant to look back upon. We'll be returning to England in a week or two, Laurie.'

'Already!' I exclaimed. 'But we've been here only two years.'

'That's a long time,' said my father. 'My work is over and I have to go back to a job in England. We'll find a good school for you back home.'

'It's a fine school here,' I said. But it wasn't the school I was going to miss, it was Anil and Kamal and the pool and the bazaar. Could my father understand these things?

'Will we come back again?' I asked.

'I don't think so,' he said. 'It would interrupt your schooling. But there is nothing to prevent you from coming back when you've finished your studies.'

'But that will be *years* from now . . .' And feeling disconsolate, I went up to my room, where I stared at the wall for fifteen minutes until I heard Kamal coming up the steps.

I did not tell him the news immediately. We got on my bicycle, riding double, and rode out of town until we reached the fringe of the jungle. Leaving the cycle in a lantana thicket, we scrambled down the hillside to the pool.

Anil was there already, floating on his back in the green translucent water, while a frog sat on the broad leaf of a water lily and croaked at him. It was only when we were all in the water that I said: 'I'll be going away in a few days.'

'Lucky fellow!' said Anil. 'Is your father taking you to Delhi?'

'No, back to England,' I said.

Anil's mouth fell open, and he swallowed a lot of water and couldn't speak for a while.

Kamal had pulled himself up on a rock. 'I knew it couldn't last,' he said quietly, turning his face to the hills.

We joined him on the rock and considered the

situation in silence. The only sounds were the splash of the stream and the warbling of the frogs. It was a drowsy afternoon; even the birds were quiet.

'Will you come back?' asked Anil.

'Some day,' I said. 'When I'm making a living of my own. I'll come back—here,' I said, looking at the pool.

'This will be our meeting place,' said Kamal. 'We'll keep it a secret pool, always . . .'

'Don't look so downcast you two,' said Anil. 'It won't be for ever. Laurie's sure to come back. Be happy, I say, be happy!'

He jumped into the pool and I jumped after him, determined to shake off the depression, but Kamal remained on the rock, his elbows resting on his knees, his chin cupped in his hands, his dreamy eyes gazing into the depths of the pool.

Anil's mother gave a small party for me two days before I left. Apart from Anil and Kamal there were other boys from the school.

For a while we were too interested in consuming the sweets which Anil's mother had made to perfection and we did not talk much about my departure. But after the plates had been emptied, there was much exchanging of addresses, promises of postage stamps and postcards from abroad, and injunctions from Anil's mother to look after my health and to work hard and become a 'big man' one day. She presented me with a goodluck charm, a tiger's claw, which was supposed to ward off evil spirits. (I still have it with me.) Then, the party over, I walked home with Kamal, through the brightly lit bazaar, past the clock tower, down the dark avenue of mango trees and up the twenty-one steps to my room.

Anil and Kamal were both at the station to see me off. After I had helped my parents to settle into our compartment, I joined my friends on the platform. Ten minutes remained for the train to leave.

'We have brought you presents,' said Anil, and he gave me a beautiful Kashmiri scarf, which had been embroidered by his mother.

Kamal said, 'I have got a very simple present for you. It is a comb to remind you of the day we first met, when you bought one from me.'

'I'll keep it carefully,' I said, putting it away in my shirt pocket. 'I won't use it, in case it breaks!'

We stood apart from the bright platform, where sweet vendors, coolies, people late for the train, and people seeing their friends and relatives off, stray dogs and stray stationmasters, all pushed each other about. It was a happy confusion I had grown used to during my stay in India. These railway stations were always exciting places. The people, so different from one another, always fascinated me, but for once I was not interested in the crowds, only in the two faces before me.

The station bell began to clang and a guard blew his whistle.

We shook hands.

'Goodbye, Laurie,' said Kamal and Anil.

I left them on the platform and entered the compartment, looking out of the window. The train had started moving, pulling slowly out of the station, and Anil and Kamal moved along with it, walking at first, then breaking into a run. Then they reached the end of the platform, and could follow the train no more, but they waved furiously and I waved back, and the train gathered speed and my friends went further and further away, two dark specks in the glow of the lighted station, and then only the

station lights were visible, and soon these too were lost in the darkness, lost in the vast formless darkness of the country.

A Letter from Kamal

Dear Laurie,

I have waited for over a month before writing to you, because I knew you would be at sea all this time and now you must be busy settling down in your new school or college. Anil and I received the picture postcards you sent us from Aden and Port Said and Gibraltar. Anil says he will write to you very soon but, as you know, he is hopeless at writing letters.

After you left, I sat for my examinations a second time and at last I passed! Now, if you were here, we would have had a celebration in the chaat shop, or a picnic at the pool. I have gained admission to a college in Lucknow, so I will have to leave this place very soon. In Lucknow I may have to continue

selling things in order to pay my fees. Anil is a little annoyed that I have passed, because now he will be left to himself and will have to look for new friends and, of course, that will be different.

We haven't been to the pool since you left, but yesterday I went there myself to take a last look at it. And do you know, Laurie, the pool had disappeared! The stream had changed its course and gone another way, and the bed of our stream was dry. There was no pool, only sand and rocks. Even the buffaloes had gone.

Anil says the pool has gone because you have gone. It was your discovery, remember. He says that when you come back the stream will start flowing again. That's like one of his mother's stories, but I hope it comes true.

Remember, you promised to come back to India one day. I know it will be many years before you can do so, but we will always be expecting you. Even if by then we are old men of seventy, with long white beards and crooked backs, we will have to meet again. And then we will go to the pool—and if it isn't there, we'll find another—and swim together as we did this past year.

But don't wait until we are all old, Laurie, otherwise we won't be able to reach the glacier again. Come back as soon as you can. The mountains are waiting for us.